These Wonderful Spring Days

Jeremy David Stock

re.press

PO Box 40
Prahran, 3181,
Melbourne, Australia

www.re-press.org

First published 2018

Australian Library Cataloguing-in-Publication Data
A catalogue record for this book is available from the National Library of Australia

ISBN: 978-0-9923734-4-3

Cover: NASA Hubble Space Telescope image of a stellar breeding
ground in 30 Doradus, in the Tarantula Nebula.

The image comprises one of the largest mosaics ever assembled from Hubble photos and includes
observations taken by Hubble's Wide Field Camera 3 and Advanced Camera for Surveys. Hubble
made the observations in October 2011. NASA and the Space Telescope Science Institute are releas-
ing the image to celebrate Hubble's 22nd anniversary. Credit: NASA, ESA, D. Lennon and E. Sabbi
(ESA/STScI), J. Anderson, S. E. de Mink, R. van der Marel, T. Sohn, and N. Walborn (STScI),
N. Bastian (Excellence Cluster, Munich), L. Bedin (INAF, Padua), E. Bressert (ESO), P. Crowther
(University of Sheffield), A. de Koter (University of Amsterdam), C. Evans (UKATC/STFC,
Edinburgh), A. Herrero (IAC, Tenerife), N. Langer (AifA, Bonn), I. Platais (JHU), and H. Sana
(University of Amsterdam)

Dedicated to Catherine, Rosie and Ed.

Contents

The Two Londons

Between one city and the other are differences and similarities corresponding to the principles at work in each. For the sake of clarity let us call one city the actual city, which is London, and the other city the dreamt city, which is also London. What is visible in each is what is represented in each. But nothing of what is at work is directly visible, but everything is indirectly, as if symptomatically, represented.

The dreamt city is bordered on its western side by the wide and gently sloping grassland of a river's flood plain. The earth is rich and fertile and the grass is healthy, bright and always in movement as it plays in the breezes that sweep and turn, and swirl up and down the shallow valley. The river, clear and blue, is small and almost hidden by the high grass. When you get closer to the river you can see how the light sparkles in the swiftly flowing water as it hurries past the city on its passage south.

Further west, out beyond this natural border, are the towns and villages that would have been swallowed up by the growth of the city but for this river. They maintain a degree of separation from the city as well as amongst themselves by virtue of the river's protection. On this, the eastern side, our side of the river, there are no such separations and the city has formed an amorphous whole.

North of the centre of the dreamt city is a major shopping street. It runs east to west like Oxford Street but is much more crowded with shops and much less with cars, buses, taxis and people. The shops have spread out across the thoroughfare, first over the pavement and then onto and over the road itself, making it almost impassable for vehicular traffic. As the traffic has dwindled the shops have expanded. And, as the shops have expanded the traffic has dwindled. Neither could be said to have started the process, or lead it. What could be said to have started the process is perhaps the feeling that a process was about to start. Then it would be only a matter of time before effects were felt.

Winding a way through the congested spaces between the shops you sense the extent to which the pleasures of shopping are always available to, and pressing upon, the city's inhabitants. The shops never seem to close and their volumes are always increasing. The increase has been cleverly hidden inside the buildings where the integrity of expensive decor has been seamlessly maintained. Only very occasionally are there the slightest signs of what has happened. A creaking floorboard in a deeply carpeted ramp running alongside a wall in one particularly large, richly stocked and brightly lit shop, indicating the presence of an expansion beyond the building's original design.

To its south-east the city seems to spread out in an immense suburban sprawl without features other than its dense housing and undifferentiated road system. There may be major and minor roads but on the map they all look very similar and the buildings are just grey masses between the white roads. Suburbs have been given names but there are no visible borders between them.

More than once I've been further out this way – to the city's port – and found myself exploring its wharves with their flat concrete expanses of loading docks and their unmarked, unfenced, precipitous drops to the deep and choppy waters below. I have found myself swimming far out beyond the port's entrance where a number and variety of ships, boats, tugs, pleasure cruisers, tankers and cargo vessels are being tossed in the turbulent swell, some queueing for entrance, some gliding in and out between port and ocean, some smaller vessels taking on water and in clear distress, other larger ones steaming past blankly, their great dark hulls cutting heavily through the water.

Returning to the city it might be better to travel west along the southern edge of the suburban sprawl. The southern border of the city is unusually abrupt as though it was walled like a medieval city, or rather was just a modern city displaying construction commensurate with a medieval fear. To go this way is a long detour but avoids the worst of the traffic on the worst of the roads. Then you can cut up to the north along a main route through the more open southern suburbs and into the centre proper of the city.

Where the rail transport system above ground is bewildering, below ground it is frightening. Below ground the trains are more like artillery shells blasted from inside a gun barrel deep inside a fortress and thrust along the dank, dark stone and metal tubes with a roar of compressed air to a threatened explosively destructive arrival that never actually eventuates. Instead the trains come to a sudden, almost silent halt but for a hissing escape of air, at the criss-crossing platforms of various unmarked and indistinguishable lines of transportation, before they shoot off again along narrow, vertiginous tunnels.

Getting on the right train is not possible. There are no destinations, only these cramped and confused way-stations on pointless journeys. It is much more like a ride at a fun fair, part roller coaster, part helter-skelter, than a quick way of navigating a city that avoids surface traffic. The only way to get out of this train system is to wake up.

Above ground the train stations are often broad, open-air areas without platforms and where as many as a dozen lines come together. Standing at the ticket office you can look down on the activity in the station as if upon a shallow, expansive amphitheatre. Trains come and go. Some stop, others do not. Public announcements have little bearing on the activity and when they do they give misleading information. Often it is necessary to board the trains while they are still moving as all they do is slow down as they pass through the station.

There are no platforms, neither are there footbridges or tunnels and you are forced to walk across the train lines, rapidly and fearfully glancing back and forth to see if there is a train coming. They can appear from nowhere, either single diesel engines or great cargo trains of many long and heavy trucks. Great masses of dark steel, cutting through the landscape, remorseless and unstoppable.

Coming down the ramp from the ticket office and turning a corner you come upon a great shed of perhaps twenty terminating lines most with trains standing at various stages of readiness to leave. Of the two or three about to leave in the next few minutes there is usually one that promises to go close to where you need to go. But this is definitely the end of the line and although you can board a train you cannot expect it to go anywhere, and the ones that appear to be preparing to leave are only perpetually seeming to do so.

Board the right train and alight at the right stop, walk along a deserted road and under a rail bridge, turn a corner, and a different kind of station comes into view. You are right in the very heart of the city now. The stations are small with single platforms and the tracks that join them have undergrowth pushing up through their sleepers. On either side is a gentle countryside of small fields, grassed land and trees. In the distance, all around, there are intimations of the city just out of view – a harsh light glancing off steel and glass surfaces – but overwhelming here is the peace of the pastoral scene. The train stations are unusually close together and barely have you turned a corner than another comes into view. The line winds backwards and forwards like this, from east to west, making 180 degree turns to north and south after only half a mile or so. It makes progress through time many times more efficiently than through space. The stations have the names of small villages in the countryside far beyond the confines of the city but here they are all fundamentally the same station and are unconnected to any place.

On occasions I have found myself lost in the northern reaches of the city, trying to get south into more familiar territory. The houses here are several storeys taller and they are densely packed together to the extent that the train lines have been built high off ground level and often above the roofs of the houses. The train moves through a landscape of slate tiles, dark stone and brick chimneys and silver television aerials. Once again there is the anxiety associated with the unfamiliar and uncertain route. I know this city so well, it is like a part of my mind, and yet always, I find it impossible to navigate without detours, delays and discomfort.

To the south west the river that opens onto the estuary is bounded by high brick walls, old and dark. When you find yourself swimming in its inky, black waters there is little to swim for at the banks, or to reach for when you get there, by way of handholds on the slippery, black stones, indistinguishable from the slippery black mortar that binds them together. Fortunately the water is unusually buoyant and just as you begin to sink beneath its placidly lapping surface you find yourself held up again.

The bridges over the river are remarkable constructions of heavy, dark steel, bolted and welded together into the most solid and complex of structures. In their centres the light only just manages to filter through to the sheet steel surfaces of the roadways within. These are sometimes multi-levelled with two sets of roads in each direction and somewhere above or below these a further level for trains. On the outside of the roadways are narrow causeways for pedestrians to cross.

These constructions are often dripping wet. Periodically they lower themselves down into the river and submerge themselves in the dark, heavy waters, before rising up again, draining torrential walls of water from their sides and righting themselves with at once massive and minute adjustments to the deafening wrenching noises of metals under massive distress and duress, before coming to some sort of rest again to allow the built-up traffic at either side to pass once more.

Occasionally greater struggles are being engaged in and the bridges creak and twist and turn with restlessness and reluctance at their burdens. But the burdens are not of traffic across them and through them of which they are barely even conscious, but the awareness of their own darkness, weight and complexity. Sections of the bridges fall away without warning, plunging into the river with great, thundering splashes and the traffic has to wait again, or risk a sudden, uncontrolled dash through the unresolved disturbance and danger.

In the city the homeless man is tugging at the corner of my overcoat. He won't let go. He wants me to stay for a while, to sit down and talk with him and his companion. I consider it for a moment. We are outside, on a raised walkway, looking out over the city skyline. I look up at the cloud-filled sky and then at the facade of the building in front of me and its place in the view as a whole. I can see the potential for beauty in everything around me, the qualities of the building's prefabrication and the welcoming softness and mildness of the clouds, and I can feel the presence of freedom, the freedom that is available here. But somehow, today, or at only this moment even, the light is not quite bright enough, the sun not shining on the windows and the walls and lighting them to quite a sufficient degree. It is all too grey, and I am not ready to reject the conventional world of security and possessions in favour of a life on the street. And so, I pull my coat from his grasp and go back into the station. Back into its labyrinth of tunnels, passages, platforms, levels, directions, detours, and delays. Enormous trains roll in and out of the tunnels and I look up at their route displays and know none of the names. They are the names of insignificant suburbs within the city and insignificant towns outside it. There is nothing familiar, nor of any meaning. None of them are any use to me and I turn against the tide of passengers moving towards them. Lost, I ask a station worker which way it is to Goodge Street, and he tells me that I'm already there and nods towards the exit. I see a blinding sunlight shining through the wide, glass doors.

Looking back now, and through the windowed doors of the station's exit and the blinding sunlight that is streaming through them in sepulchral rays, I am intensely aware of the feeling of freedom that I was offered for a moment in a life on the streets and rejected in favour of having a house or a flat in which I could keep and add to the quantity my belongings. In refusing the opportunity to abjure this acquisitive wealth and owning nothing more than the clothes I stood up in I was also aware momentarily of the riches that were available to me on the street, in the city. In its buildings, its architecture, in its sun, wind and rain, in its cold and heat, in the sky and clouds against which it stood, the light and dark that washed over it, and it sank into, and was drenched in and saturated by, in the ebbs and flows of its traffic, the turbulence of its constantly shifting population, its order and its disorder, its invitations to read it, its resistance to its reading, its minutes, hours and days, in all of this, I could stand and walk and sit and lie down and be free.

Departure

Standing reserves

Only a few of the most minimal requirements were met in the standing reserves. By the time that had been set as a deadline arrived – at which it was to be decided whether to continue with or abort the departure – it was already too late. Many of the criteria for setting this deadline had either fallen short of or exceeded the expectations they carried – for them time had either raced or dragged – what was hoped for was disappointed, what was feared was faced and then there was no alternative but to carry on.

Questions had been asked of us that we could not hope to answer. Decisions were made on the basis of what were clearly just a few predictions. A certain shelter had been afforded by the expertise of professional practitioners – that expertise which was imagined, that which was projected, that which was expected. So few know the story of the education to this expertise – its origins, its history, its telling events – and fewer still its motivations, intentions, hopes and dreams and its illusions. There is a painful drivenness, a compulsion, a search for recognition, acceptance, credit, love, that it is always too slow or too late to find. And of the time and place arrived at, the conditions pertaining – the slips, twitches and involuntary movements of a reasoning so highly trained, and so confident and so prepared to countenance a certain level of risk, the consequences of which it knew responsibility could be borne with the clear conscience and that particular equanimity of professional distance – none were wise.

Cargo cult

There is the faith and the belief, the messianic promise, of salvation in particular, as the remnants of humanity drift through space in their cargo ships. Having left their spent Earth generations before, they live now infused with a religious belief and a fervent hope that at some time in the future, generations hence, they will find another planet with air to breathe, water to drink, nature to live within, rather than be here, in cold, inhospitable space, within their harsh metal boxes in which they must seem to have died and yet live on, sustained by the technology that had brought them to this pass and to such an unmistakably primitive worship of Earth to come, a second time.

Distinct entities

Prior to the final breaking apart of these two now very distinct entities there was a period of terrible oscillations between the extremes of it being essential that they break apart and equally essential that they stay together. Had there been a blade attached the entities would have been cut to pieces and their separation or not rendered immaterial. But it was with a blunt instrument that each successive blow was delivered and the entities, though bruised and bloodied, remained intact. It was thus assured, that when they did finally separate, it was with equal parts relief and despair. For example: a people from its planet, partners from each other, discrete units from the continuity.

The effects

When you come to an understanding you do not eradicate the effects of your previous lack of understanding. Precisely those effects remain. When you come to an understanding, as if to a place, you bring with you all the experiences of all the places you had passed through together with all the emptiness of there often having been no such places, none of which consisted in understanding. When you come to an understanding, you neither pay for it with any of the benefits of not understanding, nor do you lose, give up, or give away, any other previously held possession, right or freedom.

What is it that

What is it that words fail to grasp if not the very undifferentiated, indistinguishable continuity from which words emerge in order to cut that continuity into pieces? The work is in pieces because that is what language is and does.

Gutter

The pavement, the street, the laneway without either. Uneven stones, a shallow gutter down the centre, various fluids mixed there. Rainwater, having fallen through the particulate-filled sky, then falling on rooftops and running down gutters. There is also engine oil and the soapy water from washed windows, walls and floors. In the process of making the kitchen floor of a small backstreet restaurant clean, the laneway outside must be soaked with a rush of water-borne food scraps, vegetable peelings, animal fats and fluids, the broken down parts of a carcass that did not quite make it to the bin. Lumps of matter turning slowly in the flow. The force of that flow weakened as it leaves itself behind and strengthened by what it finds. Success makes no more sense than failure. I would not stop. I could not stop. I had no reason to stop.

Progress 1

The invention of the science fiction of suspended animation serves only to attempt to evade the truth of people having to live and die in space in what otherwise would be an intolerable state of waiting. It encourages us to hope and believe that immense stretches of time can pass with no-one having to be conscious through it.

Instead, the truth is that the waiting will have to be observed and endured. The vigil will be an ordeal without equal in the past. It will make all previous diasporas, pilgrimages, purgatories, wanderings in the desert, seem like children strolling along a riverside path.

Equipment

How much more complicated it is to do anything when the way you do it is determined by the security and protection you afford yourself against the painful effects of failing in the process of doing it.

For example, climbing a slippery pole with all the paraphernalia of ropes and spikes, crampons and pulleys, harnesses and nets, as against using only your bare hands and feet.

Forme

There is a small site perhaps a hundred miles in diameter, towards the centre of the continental land mass which is cleared of all people and its border secured. Attempts are made to break through the border and enter the site. It is immaterial for what purpose or with what success. It is determined that the border should be made more secure and so its patrols and watchtowers are extended into the site's hinterland. A security operation is put in place seeking to uncover in advance attempts to enter the site. The site is thereby defended from within an ever broadening area. Those attempting to enter must take precautions earlier and earlier. Their precautions are intensified in the ever-expanding proximity to this border. Watchfulness and care must grow with each passing moment.

We have certainly

We have certainly failed all hitherto existing revolutionary principles. Proof of this will come when it is too late, by the supersession of our own intentions and will by the next, and now inevitable, revolution to come. This revolution will occur without us. It will not require our input. It will not need us. In fact it is a large part of its character that this revolution will occur in this way and to this end.

Not only will this revolution bypass us and occur without us it will also do without us. Subsequent to this revolution we will be superfluous. It will surge ahead. It will make unstoppable headway against all its adversaries. It will overcome all problems. In the future this revolution will sweep across the universe, its progress unhindered and victorious.

At this point we might come to understand that revolution as such was never ours to make but instead that for a short period in universal history we had been its flawed guardians, inadequate to be its custodian for any longer a period of time, but momentarily and necessarily a refuge and last resort for the minimal defence and keeping of its principles, if not their development and realisation. In nearly everything of this kind we will be seen to have failed, except in this our role as such minimal carers.

It's not a matter

It's not a matter of what you can understand. It may not be a matter of what you can grasp, but rather a matter of what you can only barely touch. And then again perhaps you cannot quite reach it but it must remain enough that you can see it, and see it closely, or perhaps only at a distance. And then perhaps you cannot even see it, it has to be enough that you just know it's there, just out of sight, but not out of mind. And should you come to doubt this knowledge, you might have to come to a belief that it's there and to have a faith in its presence, near or far. This faith too will be subject to doubt, sometimes it will be lost and what will remain is just a hope and then, not long after, a hope for a hope yet to come.

The living

The living can be far away but the dead are always close.

In any given river

In any given river there is a point without dimensions. It moves in the currents and flows of the water, in its eddies and whirlpools, tossed and turned. At any given time the point can be joined by others in a succession of points, before and after, and a line is formed, a line with a single dimension of length. And it in turn moves in the currents and flows of the water, twisting and turning. The line can be joined with other lines and together form a plane with the two dimensions of length and breadth and it in turn will twist, fold and slide in the currents and flows of the water. A group of planes can join and become a volume with three dimensions of length and breadth and depth and roll and turn, and at its various times and places its body can be distended and compressed, growing and shrinking, formed, deformed and reformed in the currents and flows of the river.

If we are

If we are to be drifting in emptiness then the very least that emptiness must be empty of is time and space.

Holloway Road

The rain drips through the broken window pane, running across the sill, reaching the edge at a single point and falling over it in a continuous silent line. Before it is a third of the way to the floor it is broken, or it gathers, into a succession of droplets, tapping out a rapid and light beat on the linoleum floor. Each splash is entirely unique, this is a fact. It would be remarkable, and perhaps disastrous for the universe, if two were the same.

A small stream runs across the floor and gathers in a pool around the soles of my shoes. I lift a foot momentarily and the water rushes beneath it. I lower it again and the water is forced out. I look away to the window. The room is not warm and I am sitting in my coat. It restricts my movements in the armchair. But my head and neck are free to turn, lift and drop. The light is going from the room and its features are growing dim. There is almost nothing to look at and through the window the greyness is overwhelming. It is as though the entire city is willing itself into indistinction.

Twenty miles to the West is the airport. Every few minutes an aeroplane lifts off, lumbering down the runway, until, with a roar of its engines, it finally, laboriously, leaves the ground, its undercarriage sagging beneath it. And up it climbs, up into the cloudbase, into the zero visibility of grey cloud, until the grey begins to lighten to white and then suddenly the plane breaks through into the day's final blinding sunlight.

I'm standing at the window. I look down to the opposite side of the Holloway Road. The shops' lights are already on. Their business is intermittent. Passersby are hunched against the rain, hurrying to get home before dark. Many cultures are mixed on this part of the Holloway Road but from the window they are a single homogeneous humanity looking forward to warmth and shelter. You've not far to go now, you're almost there.

I place a square of cardboard against the broken window pane, tear some masking tape from a roll and stick it in place. I drop a cloth onto the floor and push it along with my foot soaking up the stream of water and the pool at its end. I sit back down in the chair. The street lights are on. The rain has eased a little. A corner of the tape lifts slowly from the glass. The lights of the council high rise glow against the darkening sky.

I take a pouch of tobacco from my coat pocket and open it. A wave of the rich, organic aroma of fresh tobacco rises up from the pouch. I pull from the edges of its mass; picking at it, unpacking it, pulling, stretching, loosening. I place it in the fold of the rizzla, add some more, spread it out. With the thumbs and first two fingers of each hand I start to roll the paper and tobacco into shape. I fold the front edge of the paper over and around the cylinder of tobacco, lift the glued edge to my lips and with the tip of my tongue run a thin line of spit along the paper. I stick it down and turn the finished cigarette a few times feeling its smoothness. I tear a piece of card from the rizzla packet and curl it over my thumbnail rolling it into a tight spiral. I insert it into one end of the cigarette where it expands out to a secure fit. I lift the cigarette to my lips and moisten its end. I strike a match, hold its flame to the cigarette's end, the paper crackles as it burns and I take in the first, long inhalation of smoke.

My left hand falls to the arm of the chair. My right hand holding the cigarette makes the slightest move away from my face and freezes there. Seconds pass, and then I slowly exhale, smoke billowing out into the room. The world slows and stills.

Everything is stopped. There are no aches or pains. There is no strain or stress. There is not a muscle, tendon or bone which is not relaxed, utterly still. The cars outside are still, the spray from their tyres held in a frozen cascade, and in every droplet the city is reflected in miniature; the streets, the traffic, the high-rise flats, and deeper into each miniature, further into the outside world, the aeroplanes hang in the night, their useless jets glowing like Christmas baubles, and the passengers are all forever locked into the back of their seats, and no-one gets away.

I may not breathe again. The will is there, and the intention, not to breathe again, not to break the spell, not to allow the world to start up again. But I know as I always know at this point that it must. I know that for this moment to exist in its very particular way other moments must equally exist in theirs. There is work to be done.

In an infinite universe

In an infinite universe that is absolutely teeming with life it must still be possible to travel forever and never see another soul.

It is a great effort

It is a great effort with great ambitions, one made largely with the aim of escaping, as if at terminal velocity, its own viewpoint. But most important, it seems, is the need to justify the validity of that goal, to laud the ambition of its aims and all at once to make a romantic adventure of it all.

The discomfort

The discomfort of all this knowledge – its ultimate indirection, its use-lessness, its waste. It must be at least as great a waste as that produced by the society that has nurtured and sustained its development. Does it have any bearing at all? Does it carry any load? This is how freedom is guaranteed. Any direction, goal or end to this knowledge would render all freedom meaningless. As if by exchange, our knowledge is rendered just so.

Refuge

I would like to take refuge now in numbers. There is a sheet of paper on which are being written rows and columns of mostly four figure numbers with perhaps some three and some five figure numbers interspersed among them where clearly some sort of extremes have been reached. Not only are these figures being written in a careful and neat hand-writing with a fine-nibbed pen, but also the data the figures represent has been carefully and accurately gathered. The figures have a bearing on our world as it is here and now. Socially, politically, economically, they have a direct bearing on our present situation. Perhaps the data reflects the changing state of mental health in our society, the extent and intensity of illnesses; its spread and distribution. Or perhaps the data reflects the occurrence of homelessness in our society, again its extent and intensity, its spread and distribution. Or, the figures represent the shifting values at the heart of attitudes to these disadvantages.

There is great care going into the writing of the figures, the drawing of the neat, precise lines and curves that make up the numerals, the evenness of ink coverage, the clear expertise and long experience of the writing hand. Also clear is the care taken in the gathering of the data, the careful following of procedures, the observation of sensible rules, the respect for the reasonable laws of science, of objectivity, of distance, of uninvolvement. It is at once a passionate and a dispassionate practice.

There is clear pride taken in the work. It can be sensed how an individuality is being served as it is defined, supported and in fact created by this activity. These endlessly shifting values then have at their centre, at their point of transcription, a quite stable entity. And this stable entity derives a great deal from its activity. The satisfaction can be sensed running through the hand and fingers, the pen and ink of this writer of numbers.

Towards the end

Towards the end, the affect derived from each instance of the obsession's relieving act is as much the memory of an affect as any actual
or real affect. Time is both drawn out and constrained in so far as it
serves the obsession, and drawn out and constrained in so far as there
is only the obsession and the moments of its acts. The memory of an
affect is still an affect, it is time that is rendered small.

We are sitting together

We are sitting together on the sand dunes behind a beach. We look
up at the sky, which is strangely dark, and its colouring uneven. As we
look forms start to appear, not quite trees and bushes, not quite flowers
and not quite grassland. Rather, in deep greens and dark blues, we are
looking at the seabed, where light reaches with difficulty and diffusion.
In its invisible currents there sways, twists and turns a great mass of
deep sea flora and all of this in the sky above our heads.

Everything is explained – the languidity of our mood, our difficulty
breathing, our struggle to survive.

The Solid State Universe

In the solid state universe 1

The radio, despite the finest movements of its tuning dial, might refuse to be tuned to the clear reception and playing of the simplest solo piano music and may just emit a most disappointing hiss. The CD player may be just out of reach, too far to drag your tired body. And the heating may be refusing to come on because of the poor positioning of the air return and the thermostat and the fact that the heating had been turned down too low earlier when the rooms were becoming too hot and moving between them picking up the kids' clothes and toys and dressing-up props and dirty dishes and cups and banana skins and plates with orange peel and pulp had become far too uncomfortable a task and every time you bent down to pick something up from the floor it felt as though your head might burst and your back might break or suddenly rigidly fix in some excruciating position and your legs were aching and your ankles and your feet and from this point you might leap –

– to what there is and how it might arrange itself –

– to a universe made of a thick, black, solid, resinous substance translucent to a few degrees, but only over very short distances. In a universe where the only form of life, with some sentience, intermittently appears and disappears and then reappears again, in the distantly separated spaces of fractures, fissures and faults, of an otherwise perfectly solid and infinite block, and has done so for all of time.

How lucky we are to live in a universe in which we can move without having had to evolve this telekinetic capability, without incurring the great cost to our materiality it would involve, and without having to undergo such a restless and endless search for a space large enough for our being and in which we might be able to freely move some part of that being.

Exist

When something becomes infinitely dispersed it ceases to exist. There is the boundary then, where and when, something is ceasing to exist because it is becoming infinitely dispersed. There is also the situation where things come into existence by virtue of crossing back over the boundary from infinite dispersal into something less than infinite and so back into existence. The sudden appearance into finitude must be like entering into life from a deathly eternity, into light from darkness, or just popping into being, like the sudden reappearance of someone you thought you had lost.

Space

All problems are more or less the problems of consciousness. All problems derive from the problems of consciousness. Like the dog, and God, consciousness too fits precisely into the space made for it.

Account

Imagine for a moment a large chest of drawers in an old house, upstairs in a back room. And now imagine the large chest of drawers has been removed. Where it stood the wallpaper is darker, its colours more intense, the carpet has a layer of dust on a rectangle of pile deeper than that surrounding it. There are the four deep impressions of the chest's feet and there are a few scraps of paper with some writing on them folded and squashed against the skirting board – a list of things to remember and a note from a friend.

Imagine this scene is a representation of consciousness and it is not the chest of drawers that is missing but something valuable you had kept for safe-keeping at the back of one of the drawers, a something that now will never be recovered.

Bullet

To some the explosion of a firing bullet may be the equivalent of a light flashing on suddenly in a darkened room. For others the explosion of a firing bullet may be the equivalent of the explosion of a heavy artillery shell. The nuances of misapprehension may be more universal than are allowed for in the structure of any and all metaphors. It may be possible to say that nothing is the equivalent of anything else at all. For some the firing of one calibre bullet may be mistaken for the firing of another calibre bullet. Only for a very few, the firing of a certain calibre bullet will be correctly identified as the firing of that calibre bullet.

Time with someone

Having spent time with someone and then left them to go home, it is particularly difficult to imagine what is going on in their minds when they are engaged in the mundane, routine acts of cleaning and tidying up and getting ready to go to bed – a time at which consciousness, as it is normally and uncontroversially understood, is at its lowest intensity. In contrast, the difficulty of such a reflection upon this minimal state finds consciousness at perhaps some of its greatest intensity – the intensity here being a matter of a certain kind of work undertaken in full awareness of the meagreness of rewards – consciousness performing its most intense work at the greatest distance and with the prospect of the minimum of success.

Half a millennium

Half a millennium after the first ships began leaving Earth and voyaging out into the cosmos, and at the time of the greatest collective human wisdom, there was a complete coincidence of that expansion of wisdom with the individual positions of each one of those ships. That is to say, the state of human knowledge corresponded to the positions of ships in space.

In the solid state universe 2

In the solid state universe there are tiny faults, fractures and fissures sometimes no bigger than a fingernail or a shard of glass. Such life as has evolved in this universe (of dark resinous matter, slightly translucent to only the shortest degree) has evolved the ability to telekinetically transport itself across the vast distances between these tiny spaces in its universe. The goal of this life form is to find a gap into which it can come to rest. All of the spaces it finds in its lifetime are too small, and as soon as it perceives this inadequacy it must move on.

The act

The act is at the limit of the thought that belongs to it. There is no position above or beyond the act from which you can look down, or back upon, the thinking that belongs to the act. There is no position of advantage, there is no better angle. There is no better angle than the one fully compromised by the single constrained instant in which it is lived.

Time slides out

Time slides out. Further towards the periphery time is more advanced, faster – like a vehicle losing traction on a fast curve – there is drift. And so time is behind, to a greater and greater degree, the closer to the centre, until at the centre time is at its origin – which, there and now at the centre, is always happening. Out at the periphery time is very far advanced indeed and at the furthest point of its reach time there and then, ceases to exist.

Any given field

Knowledge of the entire field, of any given field, can only ever be an intuition of its being a field – not a field that is two-dimensional – a field to be sown, nurtured and harvested, but three-dimensional, a field of variations in some force. Any account that seeks to introduce, or any education that seeks to teach, can only ever be a path through that field, a single line through the further dimension of time undertaken by teacher and taught at what is, in practice, experience and fact, only ever a single but shared moment of many forces.

The intuition of this limitation comes as a breakthrough in your knowledge of that field. Thereafter everything becomes more complicated. Thereafter you will have the benefit of having had a glimpse of the real complexity of the field. Thereafter you will only ever be the giver or receiver of warnings that in the limited time available only the barest introduction is possible.

The commodity

In the freedom of choosing and buying a commodity, that freedom consists of the insertion of a distance between the free position and the position which is not free. The commodity is a thing produced to create that distance. A solid wedge in its functioning, but in fact an emptiness, and working better for being empty. It is an emptiness that comes at a cost – an exchange of working time for the freedom of opportunity to make an exchange for space – this empty space – and this particular freedom. All this known as the commodity and its being nothing more substantial than a desire for something, a desire for this particular nothing. A desire for the empty space in which freedom is realised for a few moments.

In the solid state universe 3

In the solid state universe its remarkable beings leap, by telekinetic ability, from one inadequate space to another. That is to say that the spaces, such as they exist, are almost always inadequate to the size of this universe's beings. When the beings find a space that is adequate to their size they emit a burst of light. In the solid state universe, its dark, resinous and translucent-to-only–the-smallest-degree substance, allows the light to penetrate only a very short way. The burst of light is always too great and so the space becomes inadequate to the being and it is forced to move on. There is a delay between its disappearing and its reappearing again – and what might be mistaken for the end of its life is just this delay – into a space that is, or will be soon, inadequate to it.

Everyone works

Everyone works so very hard but none work harder than the unemployed. The unemployed work without the benefit of job, career, or pay. They work without the benefit of any of those distractions. The unemployed work with the hardest material known to man. Making rock-breaking chain gangs look like children in a sandpit, the unemployed work solely with time. Anyone who knows long-term unemployment first hand appreciates the ersatz nature of all other work in comparison. The unemployed, among all of us, are closest to the real nature of work. Every morning they wake up and as the day rises before them like a sheer cliff face, every moment of every day, on behalf of all of us, they ask the most pressing question "What are we doing with time?"

Inversion

The word 'inversion' does not do justice to what is happening. It is not just a matter of being turned upside down, there is much more going on. At the very least something of the original position survives in the new position, and then there is the coming into and going out of the infinity of positions within the transition from one to another of the stationary positions. There is moving too fast and there is moving too slow. There are the feelings associated with every stationary position. How long have I been here? How long will it last? Will I be here forever, or only for a short time yet? Is it time to move or should I stay? What am I to do? A breath of wind would do for any remaining coherence. Such turbulence as this can only make a triumph of a simple inversion and this is our achievement.

Instrument

Finely wrought or pedantic, according to your point of view. But if it is a point of view and we are free to pick and choose our origins and thereby declare our essence or nature to be one thing or another then the distinction between finely wrought or pedantic makes no difference. It is an instrument for nothing.

In the solid state universe 4

Time is solid. Not like stone that can be sculpted nor metal that can be heated, bent, beaten and twisted, but like resin. At an earlier stage of its production it had been liquid, but now, in its finished state, it is solid and it can never go back. Any thing of any size only has one spatial location, or, from one, up to and including, an infinite number of spatial locations, as what is thought the measure is the measure. Any thing of any duration only has one temporal location, or, from one, up to and including, an infinite number of temporal locations, as, again, what is thought the measure is the measure. Hit it and the hammer bounces back.

Disturbance

There is a category of mental disturbance the cause of which occurs only once and as such it can never be re-cognised. The effect of this one-off event reverberates down through the life of the organism as an increasing intimacy with something unfamiliar, unknown, unrecognised, a matter of which knowledge can be sought but never attained.

Like the effects of an endlessly reducing number – when it's time to go the number runs down suddenly. What had seemed like an extraordinarily large number turns out instead to have been an extraordinarily fine measure of what was not very large at all.

In the solid state universe 5

The resinous substance of the solid state universe has poetic resonance partly due to the literal and actual resonance-deadening effects of resin and partly due to the differences in its nature to stone or rock. The latter are rendered liquid by the action of time but as the sounding-bell of the requisite metaphorical qualities, resin is not. It was liquid, but once it has been allowed to set it can never return. At the end of the existence of the universe everything is in this solid, resinous state.

Curing 1

In order to effect a cure and particularly a lasting cure the treatment must also be lasting. It must be long and consist entirely of small, often uncomfortable, sometimes painful steps. There is no running in the clinic. There are no short-cuts or giant leaps, no sudden moments of astonishing progress or anything sudden at all. The greatest leap forward is to understand that there will be no great leaps forward. It is all, and always, slow. It is all, and always, one step at a time. It is all, and always, a matter of feeling to the full every quantum of discomfort, and, in such a way, of effecting a cure and making real a goal that is also a barrier to its own achievement.

In return

In return for declaring our lives and the lives of our children 'terra nullius' – open and available for the exploitation of those who are able to – we are handed a few trinkets such as a little money with which if we work hard enough we can buy food and shelter and a few more trinkets such as a little individuality, with which we can buy a little space for ourselves. If we work a little harder we might be allowed to think we have a little career and that we are advancing ourselves in the world of our fellow man and of course in contrast to and in competition with our fellow man.

Curing 2

The genuine cure moves at one tenth of the speed of the other, false cures. It moves slower and becomes more successful. It moves at one hundredth of the speed of other treatments, and then at one hundredth of that one hundredth. The perception of movement, of progress, is long gone and now is just a distant memory, and yet it is curing more surely than ever.

Curing 3

What does it mean to believe either that repetition strengthens a message or that it weakens it? Or rather, can it be said that it's known full well that repetition weakens a message but it doesn't matter because the more a message is weakened the greater the humiliation of its receiver when they are finally forced to accept it? The longer they resist, the more it is repeated, the weaker it becomes, the greater their humiliation. The message is trivial – it always was.

Curing 4

We arrange ourselves, straightening our clothes where they are twisted, flattening them where they are creased, loosening them where they are tight. We organise our limbs, our thoughts, our feelings, bringing them into the foreground or putting them in abeyance, examining them, substituting them, blocking them.

The cure is painfully slow. Each day that passes seems to prolong its course rather than bring its end any closer. The announcement that was promised, informing us of its progress, is itself postponed and is apparently more distant every day and this too is part and parcel of the cure.

Crises

Crises

Crises are a valuable part of any enduring system, the ability to weather them certainly, but far more importantly the ability to generate them and especially the compulsion to do so. Repetition, addiction, self-destruction – essential parts of any enduring system.

By increments

The year is far advanced. We are travelling as close to the speed of light as our technology at this time will allow. There have been some incremental advances in the rate of our progress and each such advance takes years off our arrival date, but nevertheless in old terrestrial terms it is as though we are in the centre of the Pacific Ocean without a breath of wind and have been so becalmed for many generations, and there is no one alive anymore who has ever felt a breath of wind, and there is no one alive anymore who even believes in the existence of a breath of wind. Now remove the ocean and the sky, remove the planet, remove the home you left behind and the destination at which you were to have arrived. You are looking for survival. Do the rats survive? It depends upon the quality of their care.

Escape velocity

Our Earth is now a dead planet and we will never see it again. It died shortly after our departure. In truth it was our departure that finally destroyed it, every drop of resource drained from it by the effort of our escape. We have dispersed in many directions. In our convoy we anticipate a journey of perhaps twenty generations. Hope is ambition at the social level.

Curing 5

Part of the cure is in the differential 'play', the loosened sliding back and forth, between the possibility of the cure and its impossibility, the slowness of the attempt and its greatness, its hope and its continual delay.

Extension

At the centre time is just coming into existence, at the distant periphery time is at its most advanced. It is an illusion of our close proximity that we all live in the same moment. All the moments of time that have come into existence are still present and all equally available to us. We only have to travel there.

When we leave this limited region of space, so small that it is barely a region at all, but rather a point without dimensions, then and only then, will we come to experience the full height and depth and breadth of time.

Sufficient reason

Is it unreasonable to expect to find sufficient reason to act from within reason alone? That is, fully consciously, fully self-consciously, to find grounds for action from within the process of rational thought – from within even a theoretically accomplished position. Or is it always necessary to make some leap – a leap of faith or belief (in yourself or in another), a leap of faith in rationality's ability to serve us, or a leap of otherwise irrational commitment – a leap born of a loss of faith, a loss of belief, a despair at ever finding sufficient grounds for action?

The ability

If you had the ability to fly you would want to be very sure of your ability lest you reached a very great height and began to doubt.

Curing 6

The enduring cure for a mental dysfunction is, to the greatest degree, a matter of endurance. The ability to endure must be fostered, nurtured and grown. The ability to endure being the cure, both its means and its end. The process of the cure is announced, and so it is inaugurated. Thereafter all there is and all there ever needs to be is this commitment to the agreement that a cure is being effected. It is not that 'time heals all wounds', that is certainly a part of it, but only the ideological part.

Knowingly

When it became simple and easy for people, individually and privately, to undertake trips into space in their own spaceships, many took up the opportunity, and launched themselves into space in a direction of their choosing, knowing all the time and full well that they would never be returning. They knew that they would continue to live for as long as they could under the specific condition of being alone.

They knew that one day it might happen, for example, that they would have a debilitating fall, perhaps between the viewing deck and their ship's galley, or between the galley and their sleeping quarters, and that if they tried to crawl, or drag themselves along the floor, to the galley perhaps, they could live for a while longer on what food and drink they could reach, or to the viewing deck where they could spend their last days looking at the stars, or to their sleeping quarters where they could die more or less peacefully in bed.

Or perhaps they could not move themselves at all and they would die where they had fallen and that would have to be the way it ended for them. Later they might be discovered by some other life form – the skeletal remains of the ship's sole pilot, a pilot who had died alone in space, but one who had clearly done so knowingly.

Assuredly

In the future when the history of revolutions is written and shows that before the last, enduring and successful revolution burst into life and spread freedom, justice and equality throughout the world, it was necessary that five, ten or twenty revolutions burst into life, faltered and died, then that is the way it will have been. It will also be shown that the part you played in any of those failed revolutions is as assured as the part you will have played in the last.

To set out

To set out, in a deliberate and premeditated way to fashion a work, without commentary, without supporting metaphorical apparatus or key, without myth or legend, without narrative, whose content might as well be a series of numbers as a series of words – but a work with a precise and perfect correspondence to the truth of the world – in a mathematical mode of accurate accounting, in the plain mode of unadorned description of what there is and how it is arranged, in the abstract mode of structures and their relationships, and in the indifferent mode, both to the cares and concerns of the reader and to the cares and concerns of those so read.

Cycles

Cycles of acceleration and deceleration in the system bear witness to
the system's vitality. Should there be any further doubt, these cycles
of acceleration and deceleration are also of varying length, duration
and intensity, that is, they are subject to cycles of acceleration and
deceleration themselves and so in turn bear witness to the vitality of
the vitality of that system. What further proof is needed? It must be
an entirely natural system.

TRRCF

That there is a quality and quantity of consciousness, rising and
falling, subject to crisis, diminished and dispersed, subject to health,
discovered and gathered. That overall there is a tendency for the rate
of return on consciousness to fall. That it be, for the successful functioning of the system currently installed, intermittently and unpredictably and cyclically, destroyed. There is a need for the periodic
and widespread destruction of consciousness.

Paths

There is the plasticity of consciousness and its flexibility. In a further set of metaphors, consciousness, in its early days, is arduous to explore, arduous to progress through and the process of learning, of acquiring knowledge, of finding a way through experience, is the making of paths – cutting through the undergrowth and compacting the earth and forming these paths along which progress becomes easier. Easier progress comes at the cost of difficulty in divergence from those paths, until, in its later days, consciousness is stuck in those deeply worn tracks and the quality and quantity of consciousness, previously defined by its ability and willingness to confront the arduousness of its progress, and the results it achieves, is diminished.

Slow water

In terms of erosion – including sedimentation, and movement, as of terminal moraine for instance, or relocation, like sand along a coastline, and including the kinds of movement involved in fracturing, splintering, splitting, breaking off and breaking down, falling, shifting, sinking – rock is just like very slow water.

Mistaken

Mistaken are those who think of their own times as exceptional. All people of all times are so mistaken. But they are also mistaken who think that their own times are the same as all other times. All people of all times are so mistaken. Mistaken are those who think it is always going to be like this. It has never been like this and it will never be like this again.

Pointing

If I look to where the pointing directs me I see a rock and boulder-strewn ascent rising towards a crest in the middle distance and then beyond that, in the further distance, a mountain range, some peaks covered with snow, some with cloud, and the highest, which gives its name to this range, hidden behind all of these and always so hidden. If I set out up this slope I fully understand that with the stones shifting beneath my feet and the boulders constantly forcing me from a straight and direct path that I will tire quickly. I have a memory of thirst, of what it is like to be thirsty, but I do not thirst. I know I should tire but I don't.

Impacts/Exchange

So far

They did not go so far as to meet. Neither did they go so far as to separate.

In order

In order to think about something it is necessary to reduce that something to very little, to nothing even, whereupon one can think about whether it is or is not.

The bigger mistake

The bigger mistakes yield the greater lessons, and the biggest yield the greatest. To be paralysed by the fear of everything is to know the universe.

The wedge

Everyone partakes of the same subjectivity and equally everyone forms a relationship with that subjectivity. Equally, it may appear that there are quantities and qualities of consciousness but it is only an appearance. One forms one relationship while another forms another relationship. Some form bonds of great complexity, others of great simplicity. Some form bonds of apparent disinterest, others of intense need. There is no variation in consciousness, which remains a constant, there is only variation in the relationship adopted towards it. Some would say this is all a mistake and the truth is that the relationship adopted towards consciousness is consciousness itself, but it's too late, the wedge has already been driven in.

Effect

The effect of certain systems is to flatten out intensities. An economy operates in which the yield effect of peak-like high intensities is exchanged for insurance against the drain effect of trough-like low intensities. You pay periodically for the insurance and continuously for the deadening of affect.

Affect

You are addicted when the economy of affects goes into recession. You are forced to seek help when recession becomes depression.

You ask

You ask a question of the work and it is precisely the right question to ask. But the work is the answer to your question and precisely the right answer.

Impacts 1

The universe is in constant search of deliverance from its rigid determinism. Towards this end it has created intelligent life. Intelligent life has the capacity to soften and perhaps absorb the impacts that are characteristic of strict cause and effect determinism.

Impacts 2

With intelligent life hitherto the universe has only had limited success, but the exact extent of that success is a matter for the belief and conviction of intelligent life alone. The universe makes no such assessments. The universe is compelled only to continue its work. The universe is compelled to continue in its mindless creation of aggregates and complexities to the extent that over time it might create something from within itself, made of itself, that might be free of itself.

Impacts 3

It is difficult for intelligent life to endure for very long. It is difficult for intelligent life to bear the weight of the universe's hope and expectation. It is difficult for intelligent life to absorb such impacts an entity as great as the universe works so hard to avoid.

Impacts 4

In the case of an infinite number of monkeys typing randomly at reckless speed and one happening to write *War and Peace* – everything that separates Tolstoy from a monkey – for example a few million years of evolution and the development of language – are blows struck against the random meaninglessness of the universe. It is the universe succeeding for a moment in escaping the lifeless oblivion it returns to at the extinction of every intelligent life form.

Impacts 5

Intelligent life has the ability to cushion the impacts of an otherwise senseless, mindless universe. Intelligent life softens the impacts by taking them into mind and caring about them, surrounding them with the work of its thoughtfulness, creativity, dreams.

Impacts 6

Intelligent life can do many things with the impacts – it is free to choose what to do with them. It can create stories, myths and legends, religions, sciences, philosophies – it can create a goal or end for them, even such an idea as a goal, is such a creation.

Impacts 7

Intelligent life is the universe's attempt to make something that is free. Free in the sense of not being bound to be the effect of some cause, or the cause of some further effect. Intelligent life holds onto the impacts, it holds on to its own life and to the lives of others, it holds on to time – to events, histories, stories. It holds on to this part of things, subtracting from them their violence, their shock and their senselessness and seeks to soften their strict determinism by a diminishing of their destructive impacts.

Impacts 8

Whether it is our smallness that calls us to a need for growth, or our sickness that calls us to a need for cure, everything about us serves to prolong and aggravate the discomfort of that growth or that cure. Even the fact that time goes slower when you are young. Even the fact that time goes faster when you are old. It is impossible to tell whether the discomfort comes from our successfully absorbing the impacts or from our unsuccessfully doing so.

Impacts 9

The universe creates life like a god, but god is a creation of such life. The invention of god by intelligent life is one part of its many attempts to absorb the impacts of strict cause-and-effect determinism and assert that there is another way, a way of sense and of meaning.

Impacts 10

The universe has created intelligent life by means of its immense magnitude and combinatory complexity. It combines and recombines in an endless, meaningless play of destruction and reconstruction, and by means of senseless impacts, that intermittently, rarely, but by such extensivity it becomes a statistically, mathematically achieved reality and that by such force of numbers, in the form of intelligence, sense is finally made and might endure for a while.

At no point

At no point, line, plane, or volume, is the integrity of that point, line, plane or volume, maintained, promised to be maintained or in any way guaranteed. Each point, line, plane or volume is in continual transition, in to or out from, its continually shifting relationship to any and all other adjacent and touching point or points, line or lines, plane or planes, volume or volumes. Also, every point, line, plane or volume, can at any point, line, plane or volume, slide between any of these n dimensions.

The movement is always in progress, transition is always being effected, no state ever endures, no dimensions can be numbered for more than an arbitrarily and only purportedly isolated moment. All dimensions are subject to all the vicissitudes of all the others to the extent that not one can be distinguished from any other and to speak of dimensions is an unwarranted simplification. Everything can be seen in this way.

Impacts 11

To avoid the charge of stoicism it is necessary to make ourselves sick, or to make ourselves small. Sick, such that we need a cure – small, such that we need to grow. These two problems are sufficient for us to avoid our claiming to be strong, or worse, our taking refuge in quietism.

Impacts 12

Whatever is thought, written, worked upon, lived-with and loved and then after perhaps no more than a night's sleep is found the next day to be bland, innocuous, trite, trivial, makes up the constitution and metabolism of our days. It is a practice, like religious observance, that is undertaken so that you can count yourself among the believers – in this case among the believers in sense.

Impacts 13

The idea of successfully absorbing an impact implies that something disappears without a trace and without a corresponding transformation – into heat, into dust, into light, into anything. It is an impact, an event, that, having occurred, leaves no remainder, especially in memory.

Cube

The elements of a room force, over time, psychic correspondences. Disturbances of irregularities certainly, but also disturbances of regularities, which are the worst. This room is a perfect cube.

Stand-in

The relationship between those who seek a cure or growth and those who, or that which, offers to facilitate such a change, stands in for any number of other relationships. It stands in for the relationship between effect and cause, but with none of the possible permutations of pairs yielding or transmitting any knowledge. It stands in for the indistinction in all relationships. It stands in for the possibility of anything at all standing in for anything else at all.

Exchange 1

One thing is exchanged for the relationship between two things. One thing is produced, the value of which is recognised and the cost of which is recovered, plus some, when it is exchanged for a relationship between two things, one of which is similar to the first thing by virtue of being a valuable thing produced and a second thing, which is a stand-in for everything that might be a valuable thing produced, but the character of which is its sliding, variable quantity, its quality of being abstract – its property of being a stand-in for the relationship between two things.

Exchange 2

One thing is exchanged for two things. One of those things is similar and the other is dissimilar. The first is similar to the original by virtue of being concrete. The second is dissimilar by virtue of being abstract, it has had its concrete reality wrenched from it, leaving its abstract remains to impact upon the relationship into which it is forced.

Exchange 3

It is the incommensurability between the two things – one thing exchanged for another – that yields what is so unusual about this interaction. It is an impossibility of the two ever being equal and nevertheless the exchange going ahead that yields these strange values.

Exchange 4

There is such an inequality at work that it can only bring about an exchange. These things are linked precisely in order to yield such an inequality. Everything is brought into and taken out of a relationship with everything else in order to yield an inequality.

Exchange 5

A discrete unit, set against the assertion of continuity, need be nothing more than an agitation of the medium in which that discrete unit is formed.

Exchange 6

Doubts and convictions about our freedom are enough by themselves to
cause interference in the continuity and give rise to discrete units – to
measure and measurability, to exchange and to relationship, for only
in the final instance for us are these things determinate and until then
doubts and convictions they must remain.

Exchange 7

The smallest measure goes to the heart of measure. The smallest
measure agitates against the continuity. Agitation is at the heart of
measure.

Abstractions

It may be easier to think of these abstractions in terms of your relationship with your partner and then in turn with the world around
you. Or, if you are without a partner, your relationship with your
home and the world around you. Or, if you are without a home,
then the clothes you wear, whatever shelter you can find from the
environment's impacts, from which homes are intended to protect
you, and partners can, and the world around you.

The branches

The branches of knowledge are not branches at all, they are vortices,
eddies, whorls, the conceptual descriptors of turbulence – of the careful
and considered dissipation of energies – of the disturbance of a too
rapid flow – of deceleration, detour, delay.

These Wonderful Spring Days

It is becoming

It is becoming clearer every day that we can no longer hope to encounter the new worlds and new lives that were promised to us when our journey from Earth began. Our progress has been dramatically delayed and we are now held firmly in the grip of the competing gravitational forces of opposing systems.

What remain to us are the decisions between equal dangers. One demands the compromise of our remaining momentum – a change of course, even many changes of course, as we would seek to probe and test the forces arrayed against us for a weakness that we might exploit and slip through. The other demands we maintain our course and so hold on to our much diminished momentum in the hope that we will ultimately break through, draw away from what holds us and move freely into clear space.

Our days pass. We have kept the illusion of our days. It's true that they are a little longer now. We adjust them to keep pace with the slowing metabolism of our progress. If the situation continues we will need to make a further adjustment, perhaps more radical and rather than react with piecemeal solutions we may find it necessary to exercise a more rigorous austerity with regard to the traditional values of our units of time. In proximity to these decisions, in facing up to their demands, we are slowing to a crawl. That with which we seek to decide becomes ever more laboured.

We have given up many things since leaving Earth some have been missed and others not, and there are some with which we are yet to find our way. There is no sense in which our social arrangements can be said to reflect the values of an individualist meritocracy. No one works for their own advancement any more, there is no sense in which we seek to differentiate ourselves against, or in competition with, each other. No one can own a house any more, or a car, or really any possessions at all.

The question of possessions extends as far as our children, the next generation and their futures. From birth, it is an option available to us to consider our children as only very loosely determined with reference to their parents' qualities – their ownership or possession of their parents characteristics. If one parent is a navigator and another a counsellor the aptitudes the child might display can be quite freely associated with those of a counsellor or a navigator, or both combined, and their amplitudes encouraged, nurtured and directed as such. But on the other hand a child can be thought of as displaying the qualities that lie on a continuity between on the one hand those of both parents, to either parent, to qualities quite distantly related to those of either parent, to qualities distantly associated, to qualities tenuously associated, and to qualities you would work hard to find presaged by either parent or grandparent or any relative however far removed. But however far you look, when you do look, paths there are, associations there can be, similarities and differences can be distinguished, made, held to and endure.

No one's work is insignificant. We live in a small and fixed area. We have had to learn to live together within such constriction. There are no territories to open up, no new lands to occupy, carve up, possess. There are no national boundaries to protect us from outside and keep us secure in a fixed and finite culture, environment, social and economic condition. There is no wealth. There is no uneven development. There is no ideological, or otherwise, distinction. There is just the ship, in space, in time, making its increasingly meagre progress.

Just because it seems difficult and complex, it does not follow that, simplification and reduction having failed, we need despair. We are able to navigate the difficulties and complexities with whatever intuition and creativity we can gather. We are able to counsel for a path that only has a weight of rational evidence behind it – a measure against the nothingness, rather than expect a conclusive proof that will remove all doubt. The associations can be rapid or slow the allusions deft or clumsy, gentle or forceful, the paths obscure, uncertain, the subjects of decision, conviction, faith or want of faith, want of conviction, just decision.

We are here and we are here together travelling through space as we have always done. We are not spinning out into the void, we are on a path. We are not fighting each other, there is collective work. The path may change it may split and diverge, it may come to an end sooner, later, for some or for all. Difficulty and complexity are in its nature.

Narrative

There are narratives that systematically deny you the pay-off, permanently postponing it, affording you glimpses of what it offers but then snatching it away. They bleed the promise of the pay-off, drip by drip diminishing it over time. You're amazed at the time that you've given to these narratives – all the time of your life. You're kept alive until the moment you no longer care and then a short time later the narratives are quietly discontinued.

TRRDF

We make distinctions – they are useful tools. We do well to remember we make them. Periodically it is beneficial to allow those distinctions to become indistinct once more. There is a tendency for the rate of return on distinctions to fall. It is necessary, for the system currently installed, that there is the periodic destruction of distinctions.

A complex system

A complex system is analysed by means of breaking it down into smaller, simpler parts, for the purpose of understanding. At some point the parts become so small that their existence at all comes into question. Whether a part is or is not has crossed the limit of our understanding. This is at the limit of our understanding of the smallness of parts.

The work of the barren period

The work of the barren period has unique qualities. Its degree of abstraction is high as is its dry, even arid, tone. Its content is diminished as is its context also. However, as long as it is understood, from the beginning, that it is the work of the barren period then its very real worth and its particular though subdued richness can be appreciated, its qualities felt as they should be and its unique character recognised as in fact exceptional within the whole body of the work.

The work of the barren period is often mistakenly neglected if not actually ignored altogether and its record expunged from a body of work as being of a less inspired, less vital and dynamic period. On the contrary the work of the barren period can be seen as indicative as any of achievement, if not in fact more indicative than that of any other period. The work of the barren period is recommended to us by the recognition of the barren conditions in which it has nevertheless endured. What is produced under such conditions is most telling.

All your strength

Hold back a force with all your strength for as long as you can and when you find you are defeated be assured the force will come back to you with all its force undiminished and now, added to it, with all your strength as well.

Quite normal narratives

Quite normal narratives merge without break or border in continuity with dreaming. To each of consciousness and unconsciousness accrues the purposefulness and the vicissitudes of the other. There is the inability to be fully awake and the inability to be fully asleep. At the heart of the most aware and wakeful narrative there is some small part that is equally at home in a dream. Each is so contaminated by that from which it seeks the greatest distance. Each resists assimilation into the continuity from which it works so hard to make itself distinct.

"These Wonderful Spring Days." 1

Three figures sit around a table in a cabin of a space ship, one man and two women. Two empty chairs. In front of a keyboard and small monitor:

(a)   "There's a projected softening of the Ariel field of 0.0116 at 1.7 degrees from the FP-4 course."
(b)   "An adjustment of 0.3, three days from that vector would not compromise us, and could offer a 70% probability of an efficiency increase at 0.25 points."
(c)   "We'll put it in the projections and see how it develops over the next 48 hours, agreed?"
(b)   "Yes, agreed."

There's a pause. (c) glances across to (a) who has not responded.
(a)   "If we adjust now at 0.1, the chance of compromise is 17% and the efficiency gain grows to 0.35 at 75%. It's in a longer time scale, but it's there. We could use it."
(c)   "We'll run the figures for a 24 hour development at both course and its adjustment."

A further pause. Tapping on a keyboard. A door slides open in the shadows at the back of the room. A man (d) enters carrying a tray of drinks. He hands them out and settles into an empty chair.
(c) outlines the discussion so far. Then:
(d)   "You know what I think of these adjustments. There's no conclusive evidence that any of them have made the slightest difference. They're all based on what are just projections."
(b) and (c) shift uneasily in their seats.

(d)   "Where's K– ?" ((e)) "She'll have an angle on it."
Ignoring the question:
(b)   "It's a matter of the weight of evidence. The Ariel FP-4 adjustment of last month took us away from compromise by the Uriel field
anomaly that could have put us back 2 years."
(d)   "Yes, perhaps. But so could any of the adjustments after that
FP-4 move, up to the anomaly itself. It's not like you're going to run
into something like that without warning – a day, two days, two hours
before."

A pause.
(d)   "We've been doing this for a while now. The efficiency trend is
downwards, we just haven't accepted it yet."
(a)   "The last cycle snapped out at 57% and hit 30 points higher
before it started to level."
Appearing to lose ground or just growing tired:
(d)   "At the time that was put down to hitting the outflow from the
Dresta Trench. We couldn't help but catch that one."
(a)   "That wasn't everyone's conclusion. Plenty of people think it's
a natural cycle."
(d) nods slowly. They drink.

Impacts 14

Intelligence is to the universe, and in so far as it is a state of being so rarely achieved by that universe, the vehicle by which environments are outgrown. That is, intelligence is an originary discordance with its environment and is created by the universe for the purpose of freeing it – the universe – from its strict cause-and-effect determinism, the latter being a law-like behaviour of injurious impacts that offers it no rest, no peace.

Forces

The secondary forces are certainly secondary. They are weaker forces, but by virtue of still being significant, still warranting the status of secondary, still on occasion having definite influence on outcomes, on intentions, on actions. Then there is the third tier of forces. Do these forces not skip a level or two? Do they not operate directly on our psyches and take possession of us as we go about our normal everyday routines? The fourth tier of forces derive as if from a historical injury, that, it is not quite clear, has either been successfully assimilated with inconvenient, latterly manifesting, side-effects or has been unsuccessfully assimilated with lasting and constant discomfort. The fifth and further tiers are at the furthest edge of unconsciousness, where their existence is perpetually in doubt.

Train

The sound of a train coming to a halt at a station – the brakes, the wheels, the tracks. The hard work of slowing to a halt a body once possessed of such a great momentum.

Boundary Conditions/Spring Days

Two ways

There are only ever two ways we can go. One of the ways is infinitely varied but for the existence of the other. We can either keep to our course or we can change it.

Domestic

Everything that goes on in the spaceship is thoroughly domestic. Nothing goes on there that does not go on Earth, but it does go on under the specific conditions of being in a spaceship, in space, a long way from Earth and without hope of return.

Space 1

Space travel is not some light and rapid jaunt backwards and forwards across space or between galaxies in which you can return home with the same ease that you left it. Space travel is slow and it is final. There is no return home.

Dawning

When light becomes matter it loses its continuity. Its movements are sudden, intermittent, irregular and without smoothness. Matter is born in these stuttering, staccato misfires. It is uncomfortable to watch as nature takes these first faltering steps towards something more solid.

Translation

This is the translation forced upon us – this ocean, this cosmos, this medium. It is cold, dark and massive, or is this just what we've brought to it?

Small

I once pursued a dream of making myself very small, nothing even, so as not to disturb the clear vision of things. By definition it was no great achievement to have succeeded.

Space 2

Space is an ocean, but one without a surface. Or at least its surface is not in any dimension we can perceive. Its surface is tightly bound, everywhere, inside its smallest measure.

Degrees

If there is a degree of freedom to be found, turbulence is compelled to find it and occupy it. Turbulence can be defined as the maximal occupation of all degrees of freedom.

Ocean 1

The ocean's surface, in so far as you can call such a thing a surface, or even an ocean... rather, it is an ocean in so far, and only in so far, as you can say it is an ocean without a surface.

Ocean 2

No rising from the depths and final breaking through the surface – no depths, unless everywhere is depths – a pressure so great it crushes everything to the smallest measure.

Boundaries 1

For the purpose of experimentation and analysis it is necessary to place the object of study in as closed a system as possible. 'Closed' means boundaries. Where the object of a science is all about boundaries, experimentation and analysis become altogether more problematic. Boundaries are everything to turbulence. The problem of boundaries is turbulence.

Boundaries 2

The flow without boundaries is the flow without turbulence. It is the infinite and eternal flow of Epicurus' rain of atoms, all falling parallel to each other into the void, without swerve, impact or encounter, without pile-up or the birth of a world.

Boundaries 3

All is lost, even the river turns away from us as though we were just a bit of raised ground.

Boundaries 4

If the problem of boundaries is the defining problem – the problem that offers definition – then the answers we have come to, fall on one or either side of that problem. The defining problem is a boundary, set between our various answers and as such a boundary it is open to all of boundary's vicissitudes. Either it is impossibly thin, like a 'now' moment, or it is impossibly thick and contains everything – everything it was thought to keep distinct.

Boundaries 5

If the problem of boundaries is rather the central problem then its centrality lends it a border from that which is not central. As such a boundary it is open to all of boundary's vicissitudes. Either it is an ever-expanding wave containing every thing or it is impossibly small like the smallest measure.

Boundaries 6

The problem of boundaries is just beyond the boundary of our past and present successes in solving problems. It is not so much the next problem to be solved as the one that will be always pushed back further by our success in solving problems.

Boundaries 7

There is always a wall, or at least there is always something to serve the purpose of a wall. It might not be so radically different from that which impacts upon it. It might even be the same thing but moving differently.

Boundaries 8

It does not lose its energy because it is isolated from the world but rather that all its energy is expended in its attempt to create boundaries between what it believes it is and what it believes it isn't.

Boundaries 9

Time that flows is subject to turbulence. Serving as the wall for time is the time that moves more slowly.

Boundaries 10

It is a matter of sensitivity to initial conditions and whatever serves as the wall.

Motion

In any perpetual motion machine worth its name its motion is trivial, very weak, barely motion at all. The closer it comes to successful perpetual motion the more trivial that motion becomes. Its success might come at only the smallest quantum of time before its motion becomes the smallest quantum of motion. Such a motion can serve no useful purpose. Its perpetuity comes at the cost of its use value.

Light

Once we have unified nature and science into a grand theory of everything it seems quite a reasonable proposition that we will find consciousness to have been one of nature's more monstrous aberrations.

Consciousness has denied us the light – the light on the surface of the ocean. It has however, or rather also, demanded that we go in search of such a light.

TRRMF

The further we go – the faster, the deeper, the smaller – the greater is the tendency of the rate of return on measurement to fall. What is the measure of our willingness to continue with this work? What is the measure of our intentions at those moments when they are most questioned? Can there be one, other than the actual outcome of the attempt to make an end? Success or failure? It is not even then that the extent of such intentions can be measured. The attempt at measurement is always futile.

Grapheme 1

With just two measurements taken, and plotted on a graph of two axes, propositions can be made about the trajectories that join them. First and simplest is a straight line between the two points and extending out before and beyond the points – a line which makes the minimum of incorrect assumptions about what might be happening, but only by virtue of its simplicity.

Second is any kind of curved, wave-like, up and down-turning line. A line with an almost infinite degree of freedom but for the two measures (and one would be enough), particularly our freedom to make incorrect assumptions about what is happening by virtue of that freedom.

But then third, there is a different kind of line. This is one that travels horizontally along the base line of the graph at the zero point of the vertical axis until, beneath the first point of the first measurement, rising suddenly, in fact instantaneously, and so vertically up to the point of the first measurement, before, but not technically before, but again instantaneously, falling vertically back down to the same zero point of the vertical axis. From there it moves again horizontally along that base line until arriving at the point directly below the second measure where it repeats its instantaneous vertical ascent to the second measurement and vertical descent back to the zero point of the vertical axis before recommencing its journey further along that base line.

In truth, the height on the vertical axis that the line reaches is both more significant and less significant than it seems. For, at any point along the vertical rise of the line, by virtue of its being instantaneous, its progress can be theoretically, practically and instrumentally halted – brought to an end – and whatever it is that the vertical axis measures, and it need not be very much at all, but could also be everything, a horizontal line can be drawn from that point, parallel to the base line. A working analogy would be of a life and the measure of its enduring.

The width of the vertical line exists as a measure on the horizontal axis by virtue of the implement that draws it – only by virtue of its being a representation.

The graph only has one upper limit. Due to the infinite divisibility of the vertical line and the horizontal lines so drawn from it the graph is no longer a line of any complexity but rather a simple, single, block of solid black. In the first case, in which a certain freedom is not exercised and what is happening is allowed to run its course, the upper limit is the highest of the two measures. In the second case, in which that freedom to make a cut in the progress is exercised, the upper limit is the lowest of the two measures. In either case the measure that is not the upper limit loses its distinction and disappears, in the first case into the empty space above, in the second case into the solid block below.

Only this construction can contain, for example, the sense of worth and meaning in the endurance of a species and the same for any one of its members. Only this construction can do justice to what might be happening.

"These Wonderful Spring Days." 2

"What possible meaning could the word 'trench' have in the suggestion that there is something corresponding to a name: 'The Dresta Trench?' Here, where we are now, out there, there are no depths that could form a trench, nor floor or walls that could demarcate a trench's limits. It's a fabrication, a fiction, a shaping of the shapeless, it's a theoretical speculation without substance."

"Everywhere is depths, everywhere is floor and walls, everywhere is trench. Trench is what it is in its best analogical presentation; 'Dresta' indicates as much that we have given it a name. The outflow gave us a tangible and measurable propulsion gain. It doesn't have to have a one-to-one meaning in precise correspondence with what might or might not be there. We've derived forces from all kinds of sources. Sources that we have given names to on the basis of past metaphorical reserves. We've never been out here before. There are no precedents. We're not following a path, we're creating one. It's true that we're making it up as we go along, but it's also true that we are going along."

"We may have gained on short-term propulsion from something we called 'The Dresta Trench' and yes, perhaps everything in between too, right up to the fact that we are 'going along'. But it is also true that we are slowing down, progress is becoming harder all the time, it may become impossible and we may grind to a halt. That is looking distinctly possible. We will freeze, or we'll suffocate, and we will die."

"Quite literally, at any moment, we could break through the forces causing our arrest. The fact that we haven't in the short term past, to the short-to-medium term past, is not indicative of what will happen in the short term future. A breakthrough in the medium term future is not an option for us it's true. Given the very unusual characteristics of the relationship between the way we measure our progress, and our views, opinions and feelings towards that progress, and the unmistakeable resources we derive from these feelings and attitudes in the overcoming of the forces arrayed against us, as well as the resources we derive from overcoming those forces that in turn support and reinforce our opinions and feelings, it is close to a pure and functional and virtuous circle of belief effect.

What sounds strangest of all but has proved over time to be effective in all kinds of situations is the assertion – made against the easily adopted and held to misconception that it is always going to be this way – is that it is not always going to be this way. We just have to work through our current difficulties and neither cleave from the commitments we've made, nor cleave to any drastic and potentially destructive action or reaction. When we have broken through, these responses to our difficulties will soon be forgotten, certainly in the way that we are experiencing them now. What the view means to afford is the vision of our ability to keep going right up until the moment when we can't keep going any longer and then at that point to redouble our efforts and keep going nevertheless and despite all the forces constraining us. There is no reason to stop. Neither is it only a matter of reason."

"Given our propensity in the past to delude ourselves, or at least console ourselves, with heavily managed stories of our valiant achievements, I was hoping we could aim for an approach that was a little more ambitious, a little more concrete. We're basically holding to the same course with only a series of minute adjustments and the rate of return on our resources in making progress is incrementally and proportionately falling. I propose a radical change of course – a rejection of the existing plans – a break with this labouriously constructed consensus view – and suggest that only such an action can provide us with a sufficient change in our rate of progress. Yours may be a purely pragmatic instrumentalism, I propose an equally pragmatic, functional, and self-conscious, act – an act that might allow us to break free from these constraining forces once and for all."

"Before we consider a more radical break from our course, I'd like to go back to the point of our being disturbed from the norm of a smooth progress and a more readily achieved consensus on the navigation of our course at that time. This was distinctly at the origin of our current disturbance and, according to another and not insignificant point of view, was equally distinctly at the transition boundary between a rather long-running stability as regards the rate of our progress, albeit at the highest speeds we had ever achieved, and our loss of patience with it."

"I think we can all sense the lines of demarcation that were felt to be so important then to be significantly reasserting themselves here and now. The complexity of incommensurables were felt then as now as a tangible force towards their overcoming. They provided a solid grounding for our progress forwards while also acting as a drag on the rate of that progress. The contradictions, the disturbance and distress they caused, were only ever forced into use. The initial yield was very strong. But almost as soon as we became aware of its forcing it began to lose its efficiency. The rate of return diminished. But we could have chosen another way. There were alternatives. We did not go into it with our eyes closed. We may have agreed to it for different reasons and the argument that agreement based on different reasons for accepting agreement was no agreement at all was put aside. The operational efficacy of the agreement was impossible to reject. In the beginning it was irrefutable, when we began to question it, it was already too late."

Boundaries 11

Turbulence fills up freedom. Freedom does not disappear, it is just an indication that it was once empty.

Boundaries 12

Turning upside-down, left-to-right, back-to-front – corresponding to the three dimensions of space – but not the final positions of each, rather the process of change between them – to which ensemble, and the whole of which, the fifth dimension of time corresponds. Between the first three and the fifth, compressed and constrained, is the fourth dimension of transition – being the one that troubles us, the one with which we are most unfamiliar and of which we find knowledge hardest to fathom, grasp, obtain – this is the dimension of transition to which corresponds the act of turning inside-out.

Random

What is random? Especially what is infinitely random? And what is truly so? The very fact that a sequence of numbers remains resolutely random denies what is truly random. True random would include periods, short and long, and unpredictably so, of order and pattern – of non-random.

True random could even be a sequence of numbers, or events or acts, that was also, even, very short and entirely ordered or patterned – entirely non-random. They might say that this sequence was non-random from the beginning, but they would be mistaken in so far as it can be or must be, according to the degree of conviction, thought of as a sequence that still belongs to the far greater set of sequences of the truly random as previously defined.

The only alternative to all sequences being random is that sequences which are separately and distinctly random and are said to remain random are not random at all by virtue of the fact that they do so resolutely insist on remaining random and as so – subject to such determination – random does not exist at all.

The sequences, for as long as they continue to endure, are forced into an ever stricter demand for the random, and the further they go the harder it becomes, and the more strictly is the law enforced upon them. The more the law is forced upon them the less truly random the sequences become. How many ways can it be said? The rule of the random is the supreme rule. The random includes everything, even the strictest and most insistent demands for the most ordered, regular and stable sequences.

Grapheme 2

The horizontal lines of the graph cannot create a solid – the vertical line is not infinitely divisible – but is rather only divisible to the smallest measure. The distinction between the smallest measures can only be of the smallest measure. Between the smallest measures of something there can only be the smallest measure of nothing. The solid block of black is neither solid nor black, it is lines of the smallest measure separated by emptiness of the smallest measure, and so, to our view, it is grey.

Dust 1

The central third is removed and in turn, from each of the two thirds remaining, their central third removed and so on, dispersing into a zero volume with an infinite perimeter, and then this much is reversed. To each one a partner is posited, separated by the width of each, the pair make a unity, are so fixed, and are posited as a further 'each' to which a further partner is posited, separated by the width of each further 'each', and so on.

A vast number of tiny blocks separated by vast expanses of space, to each partners have been posited, and in the vast expanses of space they are very close indeed, but they are still separated. As each is then thought of as a unity and has a partner posited, and the process is repeated, gradually the vast expanses of space that had previously separated these growths are filled. Where we are positioned now, space seems to fill all around us with these blocks until the moment when, beside us, we become aware of the presence of a single sheer face of a single block stretching as far as we can see.

One third of the universe is filled with a single block and opposite it, filling another third, another block. This pair now only await the positing of their unity.

Natural

It is perfectly natural that in striking the bedrock of our coming to know the fundamental constituent parts of the universe that the experience of that moment in the progress of our knowledge is indistinguishable to us from those moments in the past when we have merely only apparently struck that bedrock and have in fact just reached the limits of what we were able to know, under the circumstances pertaining, with the resources we had available to us at that time.

The limitations we felt then will be felt again, and even more so. For, at the moment of that success in coming to know the fundamental constituent parts of the universe, we will not know that we have succeeded. What will be finally telling for us – how we will come to know – will be the lack of progress we make after that moment – after striking that bedrock. That is, we will only be able to know that we have achieved knowledge of the fundamental constituent parts of the universe when we realise that our progress has come to an end.

"These Wonderful Spring Days." 3

"We're rehearsing positions we've rehearsed many times before. The final performance never comes and it would only be the more or less competent representation of a emptied-out subjectivity anyway. So much of what we're experiencing in this situation has eroded the sense of a construction of anything so coherent. We're no longer in the business of constructing individuals. Our past knowledge and use of what we have and what is available for use, and even for 'having,' has been determined and distinguished by the anachronism of this possessive individualism. No part of this construction is valid any more: not the individual parts, nor their conjunction, not the possession of fixed, stable, or solid positions, nor their competent or otherwise performance, nor, in this or any such representation, the degree of any success or the rate of any progress."

Dust 2

Progress now demands that each new theory is increasingly incomplete. As we approach the final unifying theory each new theory is full of holes. Like Menger's Sponge dispersing into a zero volume with an infinite perimeter or boundary. This image can then be reversed.

As we approach the final unifying theory our progress slows, our work becomes ever more laborious, our achievements finer and harder to gauge. Local theories in the vicinity of our position yield less and less. They seem small and weak, but the hopes resting upon them continue to build.

Stories

It is the stories by which we know ourselves – yet knowing turns out to have been a much smaller part, and a part much larger, than we had ever imagined in any story.

There is

There is that which registers in a representation and there is that which does not.

Boundaries 13

To know is to isolate – to isolate is to posit and impose boundaries. These boundaries are privileged in the sense that we make them and because we think they're innocent, or innocuous. We prefer them to have no influence or effect.

The insoluble problem of turbulence in the dynamics of non-solid media arises from the presence everywhere and at all times of boundaries. Turbulence is the effect of boundaries within, as well as at, the boundaries of dynamic non-solid media – a solid medium is a projectile – a stone, a bullet, a missile.

We can imagine, create and impose our over-arching boundaries for the purposes of isolation, experimentation and knowledge, but what we are really doing is adding a few clumsy, man-made boundaries to what are already pure and infinitely subtle boundaries and their effects – boundary effects through and through.

Ignorance

A little ignorance has gone a long way. It's too late to go back, we've come too far and too fast now to pretend the ground we've covered can be better known, respected, understood.

Links

All the links are direct, there are no indirect links. Everything is connected, and it means that in one way or another, and in however small a way, everything is known.

The large scales cannot effect the small more than the small scales effect the large. Each impacts back upon the other with whatever effects – absorbing, dissipating, disturbing, animating. There can be no inequality here.

Fluid dynamics

There is the representation of the rapid flow of water in a narrow pipe – a standard problem for engineers of fluid dynamics. There is the difficulty of the representation's open-endedness. In forming the representation of the problem, how much of the pipe do you picture? What length of pipe would be adequate for the analysis of the problem? And what is at the ends of the length of pipe that you have pictured?

In representing the whole of the analytical apparatus, including its parameters or boundaries, it is as if at the end of the pipe section nearest to us the water appears, as a creation from nothing – a jet of fluid sucked from mid-air into the mouth of the pipe, where the flow is then constricted into the thick, dull grey, steel pipe, the mouth of which is roughly hewn, its edges serrated by the picture's cut-away. From the end of the pipe section furthest from us, the jet of liquid is expelled and disappears into thin air with the same sudden open-endedness, and what had appeared to be creation from nothing becomes as if dispersal into nothing. Between these points the flow enters the experimental set-up, the constriction necessary for its close analysis.

There are then the limits of the apparatus – of the analysis, the experiment, the thinking and the representing, and the knowing – whatever knowing we might glean. It is in the behaviour of the water in the pipe that we are supposed to be interested. For the engineer of fluid dynamics it is how thick the pipe has to be, how strong and how durable it is necessary to make it to contain the water, how fast it might run, how disturbed it might become, how much strain and distress its disturbance might cause, so that nothing, none of it, fails.

Intimations

If only intimations they are, intimations they must remain. You cannot affirm an intimation, you can only deny it and hope that no-one believes you.

Interpretation

Interpretation is successful at the moment of, and only ever at the moment of, translation. Translation, previously thought of as so problematic it was hardly worth the effort, is now central to any successful interpretation. By successful we also mean transmitted and understood.

Foundation

The formation and deformation of clouds – the formation and deformation of winds – the formation and deformation of ocean currents. Of all the problems that have been found to be too complex to solve by mathematics, even with the immense and ever-growing powers of computing, the above are a few examples of the problems which – in space – we will no longer wish to solve, but rather, we might wish we could recreate.

Peace

It is fitting for the universe to create a form of life possessed of an attribute such as intelligence. Intelligence is an attribute that leads the form of life that is its possessor to emerge from its environment, a local part of that universe, and in growing and thriving, use up that environment and so be forced out of the local into the general where it might do its work on a grander scale until one day it might bring the universe some final and lasting peace of some kind.

For the purposes of our understanding now it is enough to conceive that the thing we call intelligence is at the most advanced point of the thinking of the universe as making progress in its development towards a goal that need not even be specified. It is enough also to maintain the idea that our human intelligence may be of a very low level relative to other intelligences, in the future, in the past, or elsewhere.

The definition of intelligence that identifies it as an expression of a self-destructive intention on the part of the universe is a necessary path to follow for a way, not necessarily a right path, but a way, like human intelligence itself, that will not necessarily be successful, that might well fail, and that there is no reason at all to believe will succeed. But it is a way that is now being taken.

The definition of intelligence that identifies it as, on the other hand, an expression of an intention on the part of the universe to cease its own cycle of destruction and construction with the creation of some impact-absorbing way of harnessing its otherwise wild and unstable energy and generating an altogether more peaceful peace, is also a necessary path to follow for a way, not necessarily a right path either, and no more likely to be manifested in and by human intelligence – an intelligence that may be already one of the universe's false starts in this respect.

These ways and these definitions need not be right at all for any further purpose than this. We need not be right at all for any further purpose than this.

The advance

The advance on space of quicksand is considerable. The advance on emptiness of something that provides any resistance at all is considerable.

The part

The part you most want is always said to fall beyond the scope of that chapter, that essay, that book, that life's work.

Transitions

Trajectory and speed

At no point or particle, substance or measure, however small, is there a point or particle, substance or measure, however small, that is innocuous or innocent, or even individual, as such, in relation to any other. Rather, to simplify further and to refer only to points, any point only has a trajectory and a speed.

For now it is optimal, for further simplicity, that we put aside the human values related to intentions, hopes, fears, dreams, motivations and their extent, their duration, their history, the qualities of that history. Is it a good history? Is it adequate to purpose? Does it have a use at all? And concentrate solely on the dynamics of this point.

This trajectory, and let's also assume its speed is constant for now, for any unchanging trajectory, forms, to another point, anywhere on a theoretical surface, a sphere. That subsequent point, on the surface of the sphere made up of all the positions it could have occupied, is where this process is said to begin again – a point that is not innocuous or innocent, or even individual, of any previous or subsequent point and this at the point's simplest trajectory and speed and without the slightest change of either.

In the middle

When an individual loses its way in the middle it can be with good reason and purpose. It might do so purely and simply as a demand put by the story – so that it can find itself again. The middle of the story being the account of the struggle against being lost. By the fact that the finding again is the substance and the sustenance and the end of the story, it is said to be a good story, a good history – and this is the case when it loses its way in the middle.

It is a great simplicity that a story be so linear and all of the thinking that has gone before of the stories appropriate to different numbers of dimensions can be equally simply wrong. Scalar, vector, tensor – three of the five levels we are still only barely prepared to countenance (the fourth being the one that is still hidden) and then only so long as they are all held together by the fifth – the one standing in for all the others that might come after – their strict chronological ordering.

Local group actions

There is a certain tendency in the local, and less so but still significantly in the regional, for group actions to form. This formation occurs in areas where group-acting trajectories and speeds can be identified as possessing certain characteristics. For example, the actions are stronger at the centre and weaker at the periphery – or perhaps that area of stronger activity is off-centre and the gradient to weaker activity is steeper to a point closer on the periphery and shallower or more gentle to a point more distant on that periphery.

The origin of these group actions is open to debate and seemingly has always been so and will always be so. At this moment now, when we are addressing these issues so directly and with such concentrated purpose, we lend our time a proximity to the centre of this particular group action.

One origin is mathematical or statistical. As if by chance, or at least with its cause unspecified, or even any effort made to identify one, as though it had none, a degree of activity appears that is co-ordinated. It need be only a very small co-ordinated activity at first. It might die out instantly. Hundreds of previous such actions may have lost their force as soon as they found it, gradually or quickly dwindling and disappearing – dying out without ever having become more than one of these momentary co-ordinations of activity, more or less unseen or unrepresented. But this one is different. For whatever reason, it attracts sympathetic action from the points around it in the local area. Over whatever period of time, over however large an area, or volume, at whatever intensity, and at whatever gradients of intensity's curves, in whatever direction and with whatever speed, it takes hold and with sufficient strength for us to come to call it a locally arising and occurring group action.

Another origin for the formation of a local group action comes from an external force. A force exerts itself upon an area, larger or smaller. This proposed area, then, need only react and does so in such a way that it can be seen to be a particular kind of action, one not determined by random movements or chance, but an action which has a certain integrity, such that we are not given cause to doubt its connection to the originating force, and by such integrity gives rise to significance or meaning. Again, the action could die out very quickly and hundreds may have done so, but this one is different. As such, other points, or areas, small or large, can be said to be led to act in the same or a similar way, by the points and areas acting beside them. Once again a local group action can be said to build, subject to the same conditions as before.

Subject to these accounts and their vicissitudes the local group action can in the same way grow to become a regional group action and then a general action. The question of what is general is in part determined by the assertion that general as general is possible, while general as universal is not, except as an end point, beyond which there is nothing. Generalised group action approaching the universal is a river turned to stone but a river of stone that is still moving, and moving with a unified trajectory and direction, and moving with all its distributed parts, geographical and historical, physical and chemical, economic and dynamic, including for example the atmospheric circulation of water vapour and rain, moving with the same unified force of all the individual forces that had been dissipated in what was previously, prior to its universality, its fluidity, its flow and its turbulence. It is a world turned to the solid state.

Order

The problem of keeping work in strict chronological order is the problem of order writ large. Work is only ever chronological. You may try to disguise its real order in favour of a latterly imposed other one but you are only ever disguising its true and original order, its order from its origin.

The problem of keeping work in strict chronological order is where to end one body of work and begin another. A break, or transition, is required – a circuit breaker, in which a flow, under abnormal conditions, is interrupted – or a transition, between two states – or a natural break – like a border, or a river, or a high and difficult, more or less impassable, mountain range.

Representation

There is the image that represents a map of the moving currents within the flow of a river or of turbulence in a pipe, and shows its representation to consist of lines similar to those that indicate contours of altitude around a mountain range with its peaks and valleys as if appearing and disappearing in and out of the graduations of its representation.

The mountain range, for this purpose, is effectively stationary in time and also has a fixed, two dimensional reference surface, that of sea level. In order to map the moving currents within the flow of a river or pipe it is necessary to freeze the flow in time and then also to take a flat slice, a surface or section, through the flow. Only then can mapping begin.

It is the case that it is impossible to tell whether a second section taken is different in time but the same in place, or different in place but the same in time from the first. The uncertainty is further compounded by the fact that it is still only sections that are being taken. Take a hundred sections, take a thousand, and you can still never be mapping, representing, or knowing, more than a few centimetres or a few seconds, or a combination of both.

Transitions

There is the problem of transitions. No account of any transition can fail to be subdivided into an infinite number of smaller accounts. The adequacy of any shortened, abbreviated or condensed account, which all accounts are, is down to the subjective disposition towards the meaning of the account – its purpose or end, its meaning as in its progress towards its purpose or end, or its meaning as in the selection and exposition of accounts and their transitions. The adequate account of any of even the simplest transitions would take all of the time available to us to sketch out a few introductory remarks about coordinates and volumes that remain, despite everything, in the static state.

The open dimension 1

There is the feeling of a very great expanse of open space nearby and all you have to do to go there is cross a very short distance. Either this or it's a very great expanse of open time that is available and waiting there and is only a very short time away. Or, even more accurately, it is a pure, clear, frictionless and undiminishing in any way – including of those who seek to go there – uncompromised and untainted by either space or time, a new and as yet unknown dimension, or just a world – one that is waiting there for us.

All of this might be mistaken and it is rather a feeling that the journey has already been made and the destination already arrived at. In the traditional view only the end could be adequate to such a feeling of promise, whereas it is the end that is precisely in question in this precisely transitional state.

The open dimension 2

Between the spatial and the temporal there is a transitional dimension. In the way that we don't understand this dimension we can make the same effort of not understanding the others. For example we might successfully fail to understand the three spatial dimensions by thinking of ourselves as inhabiting a flatland or even a single, individualised point. For example we might successfully fail to understand the temporal dimension if we can think of ourselves as free from the impacts of cause and effect.

The open dimension 3

Whether it is or is not depends solely on where and when it is sliding above or below the contour of our attempt to represent it. A contour drawn in good faith that is consistent and law-abiding – albeit a law of a self-limiting nature, one constraining us to making our mistakes consistently, in good faith, and successfully.

Mechanisms

They would stand by their massive and silent machines wondering why they would not work. It must be something simple they would say. It might be something as simple as flicking on a switch. The machines are completely dead, or asleep.

Or it might be something complex they might say, a diagnosis so opposite it seems that they would have to go right back to their drawing boards, even further than that, they would have to reassess all their presuppositions about their machines – where does their power come from, how do they provide drive, what work do they do?

On the other hand, if the problem is indeed simple but you can and do still ask these questions then the answers could also be simple, single words – words like hope, belief, faith, dreams, desire.

Construction 1

The same constructions invite the substitution of key parts with alternate parts which change the constructions certainly. Neither do the parts need to be the key parts, they can also be peripheral, they can even be superficial, the colour of the constructions, the degree of their shine, their newness, how much dust settles upon them – the purely local, the unremarkable remarked – that which otherwise would be a detail then momentarily a key part – or perhaps confused with something other than what it is – so simple are the things said and so convoluted their saying.

Construction 2

If a part of the machinery is a very long, iron, connecting rod beginning at one point with a lever and ending at a distant point with a switch, perhaps across the width of a room or across the width of a galaxy and then continuing on to the next galaxy and perhaps across the universe, and painted with a high gloss, black enamel paint and quite thin, but thick enough to maintain a certain strength, and the lever is pulled, there is no delay before the switch is flicked, there is no information to be sent, no message to be delivered, no mysterious communication, no movement faster than light, no teleportation, it is just a lever, a connecting rod and a switch. All that is necessary is to find the dimension appropriate to such a construction.

Collapse

Is there really a chance of psychic collapse? Can there be such a thing or is it not always the case that at the moment of collapse some other construction will suddenly leap into place as though out of thin air and assert itself, so pointlessly, as something else to hold it all together? Regardless – regardless of whether it is continuous or broken – it is a construction so fragile that it's continually threatening to fail. It's a construction seemingly designed to collapse, at some time in some way, but for now and perhaps always, will continue to do the minimum required of it.

Advance.

It is possible that in the future by some great technical advance we might achieve a testable and provable indication of the existence of an after-life, albeit of a very short duration, perhaps only a few seconds, but nevertheless a scientifically proven after-life.

Not long after this success it would be reasonable to expect that with a further advance of our technical capabilities we could extend the testable and provable duration of the after-life, perhaps for as long as a few minutes.

Thereafter the third great advance would be, as the third occasion often is, some sort of culmination of the story, and on this occasion show, as the duration of the testable and provable after-life is extended to hours, days, weeks and years, that it still could not be said to have had, nor even ever promised to have had, even the slightest impact on the duration of life, let alone even come close to addressing the quesion of immortality, but had rather only extended the duration of an after-life in the form of a half-consciousness, a twilight half-life, where, freed of the pain and suffering of what had killed it, or the state in which it had died, it was only a matter of dealing, a little or lot longer, with the experience of actually dying.

The scientifically verified after-life does not leave life untouched. It does not leave science untouched. The life sciences will thereafter be mirrored, repeated, albeit indistinctly, in a dulled way, by their twins in the after-life sciences. The physical, or hard sciences too will be irrevocably altered by the fact of existence continuing into this non-physical realm.

Also, it would never be certain whether the technical advances had become able to detect the existence of an after-life that had always been there or had actually created it. The first possibility would a tragedy as so many had died without the company and contact afforded by knowledge of an established after-life. The second possibility would be a tragedy as few would then be able to deny their loved ones this last form of life, however diminished and drawn out, and its end delayed by what would almost certainly be an expensive medical intervention for which the way would then be open for the making of fortunes for those in position to commercially exploit it.

Movement

We just move helplessly from one day to the next, without real direction or purpose and only deal with what it is that movement – our only movement – brings us, puts in front of us, and forces us to deal with. We do not generate any movement of our own, we do not dispense, dissemintae or disburse anything – we force nothing, but are only forced – forced this way and that, while half-conscious we hope and half-conscious we dream, of not suffering this or any other movement at all.

Synthesis

No great work of synthesis need be undertaken – partly because of the enormous effort required of such a focussed task and its very high likelihood of being flawed in some part, either near to the beginning so everything after would be inherently wrong, or near to the end so everything that had been achieved before would be lost, but also, and mainly because, the work should always be piecemeal, fragmented, partial, precisely unfocussed, vacillating, equivocal, hesitant, humble, always aware of itself being not a great work at all but rather only a small contribution, a work never properly undertaken, only dabbled in, as you might the occult, or a hobby, like stargazing, a passion but never a profession, part-time never full-time, unfinished, unfinishable – somewhat similar to the relationship of science to life, or nature.

Turbulence

There is an image of turbulence behind a rocket giving ground to its thrust.

Crisis

In a crisis there is nothing. Before the crisis there is the fear of what will happen, after there is the struggle to deal with what has happened. There is being disembodied – and there is being embodied to the exclusion of all else. There is standing beside and there is being at a relatively short distance and there is being at a very great distance. There is a longing for more peaceful times and a hope for the end of moments of crisis. But in the crisis, actually within it, there is nothing.

Completion

Self-completion, so completion, is not possible, so essential. Growth, or well-ness, entered into, so now in the realm of the hoped-for, makes necessary this third course of completion. From the necessary it moves quickly into the impossible – entering the realm of what was most feared it moves accordingly into the essential.

Navigation

Navigation through the theoretical field is effected by a certain control of the definitions of its terms. The control need not be sure, confident, expert. It need not be anything in particular. There is also our guidance through the meaning of its terms, and again it need not be characterised by any particular guidance and certainly not an all-knowing, all-seeing one.

If there was a better guide to this moment, the last and the next, I do not believe, will not, nor ever have believed that there is, was or will be, neither do I believe there could, would, or should be – least of all is it an ethical issue. It is neither a narrative by which we might know ourselves nor a knowledge by which we might know the world and beyond.

Comforts

There are three comforts we traditionally afford ourselves in our narratives of travel in space, of this kind of progress in time. One is suspended animation in which we needn't be awake, or aware, while we travel for years, decades, centuries in search of a destination. That is to say the first comfort we afford ourselves is that we can make progress without consciousness. The second comfort is that there is a destination and we will succeed in arriving there. The third comfort is that one day we might be able to return home.

Enduring

So that something might endure for more than a moment – a moment which defines its enduring and an enduring which defines that something. So that something might exceed itself and its finitude and continue to do so for more than a moment and so rush ahead of these its definitions – its definitions as expressing its constraints, its limits – and so that something might awaken and arrive and then at last be free to begin its return.

According

According to what you are, is where you are, when you arrive at a point, if you ever arrive at the point, at which you are prepared to believe you are mistaken, to such a degree that you could call yourself deluded. You do not fail to suspect you might be deluded, without actually knowing for sure. You do not yet readjust your set of beliefs. Rather, according to what you are, you examine where you are. Can you contain this contamination of your beliefs? Can they be easily readjusted to accommodate the new arrangement? How can normality be maintained? There is certainly a pressure to be quick – if not to be quick then at least to be certain. But nevertheless there is delay. To some it is procrastination, to others hesitation. To some it is deliberate, to others disingenuous, dissonant, dissociating, disappointing, despairing, defensive, evasive, the list is very long. Rather than adjust what you know, rather than adjust the settings of what have turned out to be your delusions, rather than attempt a truer true, a righter right, a mightier might, rather than attempt any improvement to the situation, you come to occupy it, without right of possession, or feeling of belonging, temporarily, for an indefinite time. You do not prostrate yourself, or even position yourself, you do not take up a stance, nor make a stand, you just come to be there, where, according to where you are, is what you are.

Construction 3

Movement through the field is represented to observation – to view – by an immensely fine and intricate framework which is suspended in the moving field. To some extent it is understood to be supported by the movement in the field, to some extent it is understood to be actually disturbing the field by its sheer presence there, as well as being inadequate to its purpose of representing movement in the field, for various reasons, but the best that can be done at the current time. It is more adequate the more complex, intricate and fine it is. It is more adequate the more sensitive it is, the more it is inclined to fragility and breakage, the more inclined it is to register everything, even the slightest disturbance.

It is a three dimensional framework of moving pointers that are directionally flexible in order to represent the movement of fluid, or any turbulent force, through the field. It is necessary that the pointers can move rotationally in any direction from their fixed position at one end of their length at the intersections of the framework. The pointers have a certain length which is a measure of their precision. It could also been seen as a measure of their inadequacy in accurately reflecting the nuances of a movement which is rarely in such a measure as such a length could represent.

The pointers are also separated from each other by the space determined by their length, priority having been given to the freedom of movement of each. Again, this space is a measure of the construction's precision. As with the pointers' length, so too with their separation. The degree of their separation is in direct proportion to their inadequacy in accurately representing a movement through the field which is rarely so separated. All these measures and their inadequacies go to make up the framework. All these measures and their inadequacies are necessary in order to make visible, or to represent, movement through the field that the framework occupies.

Half-knowledge

Half-knowledge, half-belief, half-desire, half-life. Half the distance to the destination. Half the story. Many millions of halves still to go.

Another world

There is a general belief, inherent in many specific, local beliefs, that there is another world, out there, somewhere, available to us, either when we are finished with this world, or more positively as a goal, end or purpose, that can be reached with sufficient of whatever it is the local belief demands – faith, courage, endeavour, hard work, patience, humility, endurance.

This other world takes many forms and comes to us in many ways – as a gift, a reward, a motivation, a substitute, an exchange, an illusion, a delusion, a curse, even as a retreat or a place to hide or just find peace. The world out there is one in which we have the qualities it has demanded of us, or, it is a world in which we receive what our already having those qualities deserves.

Time and time again

Time and time again we come upon this limit which is our slowness, albeit at the maximum speeds allowed by the laws of physics, or not unrelatedly, our insistence upon there being another world available to us – if only we could go fast enough, or be big enough, or small enough, or well enough, to go there.

This and another

It is a strange place to look for something in a single alternative. But on the other hand to deny there is only this and another and look for further alternatives, create them, to follow them, inhabit their ambiguities, is a response to this strangeness but not an answer to it, or an escape from it. Only the two remain, this way and another.

If time travel

If time travel became possible, those for whom it became possible might travel forwards in time to see the results of its coming into use, only to be dismayed and disturbed enough to then travel backwards in time in order to delay it.

Completion

It is always the goal of the longest, hardest work to complete that work, perhaps in the form of the invention of a machine or a technology, in order to bring an end to that work so that the effort of that work might be avoided next time.

It is always the goal of the most difficult and concentrated thinking to complete that thinking, perhaps in the form of a formalism, a logic or a set of rules, in order to bring an end to that thinking so that the effort of that thinking might be avoided next time.

Progress

Gradually, coextensive with our progress, it is becoming increasingly apparent that the truth of our time and space are not as apparent to us as we had thought them to be. Gradually, the observationally verifiable world we are advancing from is dissolving and dispersing. We can remain aware of the reality around us but we cannot pretend that the shadows are not encroaching. We are living in pools of light, closing in around us. As we spread about the universe, in the glorious success of our species, we can only expect these pools of light to diminish to points.

Solid

When it is the case that in a local area of space, and only in that local area, everything there is moving in the same direction and at the same rate and there is no turbulence, or boundary effect, then that local area is a solid. This is what a solid is – everything moving in the same direction and at the same rate – ruling out turbulence and ruling out boundary effect – which amount to the same thing.

Evidence

The evidence you can see might be only a very small part of the story and lead you to conclusions that are completely opposite to those that would be the case if the evidence you could not see was available to you. The reason you cannot see this evidence is because it has been destroyed. The evidence you can see has been left unharmed by the force of that destruction leading you to believe the destruction is not so extensive as it is.

As soon as

As soon as the parameters are established, the subject tends to the infinite. As soon as the parameters are secured/once the parameters are secured/if the parameters can be secured.

The parameters can never be secured and so the subject continues to be constrained.

When

When the terms are fixed/when the rules are fixed, whatever it is that tends to disperse, has an experience it has never had before of a distantly perceived freedom – on the horizon/at the border/boundary/ perimeter – knowing that the centre must go to that periphery in order for the goal to be reached and freedom attained.

Make a move

Make a move towards freedom and it recedes, not by some nightmarish shadowing force but because you are at the centre, and freedom is at the periphery – when you move, the periphery moves. Not so distantly related is having recourse to the unconscious, by which you address a part that is not quite so central.